FLAT STANLEY's
WORLDWIDE ADVENTURES 14

On a Mission for
Her Majesty

On a Mission for
Her Majesty

CREATED BY **Jeff Brown**
WRITTEN BY **Kate Egan**
PICTURES BY **Macky Pamintuan**

HARPER
An Imprint of HarperCollinsPublishers

Library of Congress Control Number: 2017932857
ISBN 978-0-06-236607-8 (trade bdg.) — ISBN 978-0-06-236606-1 (pbk.)
Typography by Alison Klapthor
17 18 19 20 21   BVG   10 9 8 7 6 5 4 3 2 1
❖
First Edition
Also available in a hardcover edition.

CONTENTS

A Royal Mission

Stanley Lambchop loved Saturday mornings. He loved waking up without an alarm clock. He loved staying in his pajamas instead of getting dressed. He loved watching cartoons with his younger brother, Arthur. And he especially loved eating waffles for breakfast.

"That's enough syrup, Stanley," said his mother, Mrs. Lambchop. There was already a big puddle on his plate.

"Okay, Mom." Stanley put down the bottle of syrup and picked up his knife and fork. The phone rang as he was about to take his first bite.

Mrs. Lambchop frowned. "Who on earth is calling at this hour?"

Stanley didn't care if it was too early for anyone to call their house. He had to grab that phone before Arthur did! Both brothers always liked to answer first.

"I got it!" Stanley sprang out of his chair. He raced across the kitchen toward the ringing phone. Arthur was already way ahead of him!

Mr. Lambchop was standing between the boys and the phone, pouring more batter into the waffle maker.

The thick batter moved slowly.

Arthur waited for his father to step out of the way.

Meanwhile, Stanley slipped around him and kept on running! He never knew when being flat would come in handy.

Ever since a bulletin board had fallen off his bedroom wall and onto him, Stanley had been barely thicker than a piece of paper. He could fit easily into tight corners and small spaces. Being flat had made him famous, too. Flat Stanley had traveled all over the world!

Stanley grabbed the phone before it rang again.

"Hello!" he said, a little out of breath.

"Hello?" a voice replied. It sounded crackly and far away. It also had an accent, which Stanley could tell by the way the caller said his name. "May I speak to Stonley Lombchop, please?"

"This is he," said Stanley, as his mother had taught him.

"Jolly good, Mr. Lombchop," said the voice. "I am calling with an important request."

"Um . . . yes . . . jolly good," said Stanley. "May I ask who's calling, please?"

"This is Detective James Bates, from Scotland Yard."

Stanley almost dropped the phone.

Scotland Yard was the most famous police force in the whole world. It was not in Scotland, though, which was a little confusing. It was actually in London!

Detective Bates kept talking. "Her Mojesty, the queen, would like your help."

"Her Majesty, the queen of England?" Stanley blurted out.

That got his whole family's attention.

"The queen of England?" repeated Mrs. Lambchop. She motioned for

Stanley to give her the phone.

Stanley tried to explain. "The queen isn't on the phone. It's someone calling *for* the queen . . ." But his mother took the phone and started talking. After that, he could only hear one half of the conversation.

"Mmm-hmm," said Mrs. Lambchop. "We could do that. The boys have a school vacation coming up."

She was quiet for a minute.

Detective Bates said something Stanley couldn't hear.

"That would be perfect!" said Mrs. Lambchop.

She was quiet while the detective spoke again.

"Yes, yes," said Mrs. Lambchop. "We will be ready tomorrow. Tip-top. Cheerio!"

Stanley knew they spoke English in England, but maybe it wasn't like the English he already knew. Stanley had never heard his mother use those words before. He had never heard *anyone* use those words before!

Mrs. Lambchop hung up the phone and turned to her family. "It's a special case," she explained. "Detective Bates would not say much on the phone. But he has an important job for Stanley. We're leaving for London tomorrow!"

Stanley was so excited that he forgot all about his waffles. He was going to spend this Saturday morning packing his suitcase!

By Monday morning the Lambchops were in London, riding on a bright red double-decker bus. Stanley and Arthur had the front seat on the top level. Stanley felt dizzy whenever he looked down. And wait—was the bus tipping over? He planted his feet firmly for support. Being flat meant that Stanley was very light. He did not want to fly out of his seat!

Arthur saw what he was doing. "Don't worry, Stanley!" he said. "The bus is only going around a corner."

Some of London's streets were so narrow, the bus could barely fit.

Stanley knew London was an old city. Of course, the streets were built before there even *were* buses, he thought.

Stanley looked out the window. Now they were passing a park. Up ahead, there was a long stone building. It looked like a really fancy school, he thought. Or maybe a fortress.

His mother tapped him on the shoulder. "Look!" she said.

Stanley turned around.

"No, not at me!" his mother said. "In front of you! It's Big Ben!"

She pointed to that same stone building. Now Stanley noticed a tall clock tower sticking out of one corner. A picture of this clock tower was on the cover of their guidebook!

"Big Ben is a London landmark!" his mother said.

Just then, the clock in the tower began to chime. Stanley counted eleven gongs of the giant bell. It was eleven o'clock! They were supposed to be at Scotland Yard by now.

Luckily, just then Mr. Lambchop said, "Here we are, boys," and the bus came to a stop.

Stanley thought they had arrived at a regular office building. Then he saw a spinning sign that said New Scotland Yard.

They were here!

"Some of London's best-known crimes have been solved at Scotland Yard," Stanley told Arthur. "Even Sherlock Holmes worked with Scotland Yard, and he was one of the greatest detectives of all time!" Stanley could not wait to hear about this case.

Detective Bates was waiting for them

at the door. He was wearing a neat gray
suit with a blue tie, and his accent was
clearer than ever. "Glod to meet
you, Stonley," he said, shaking
Stanley's hand. "So hoppy to
hove your help!"

The Missing Ring

"This way to the lift," Detective Bates told the Lambchops. They followed him down a hallway and into an elevator.

"I think the 'lift' must be the elevator," Stanley whispered to Arthur as they were whisked to the twentieth floor.

"Come, hove a seat in my office," Detective Bates said, inviting them in.

"Would you like a spot of tea?" he asked Mr. and Mrs. Lambchop, pointing to a tea set on his desk.

What in the world did he mean? Stanley wondered. The tea cups had no spots on them at all!

He could not think too much about this question, though, because Detective Bates started explaining why he had called them here.

Detective Bates cleared his throat. "As you may know," he began, "the queen of England is no longer young. When she dies, a new king—her son—will take part in the traditional coronation ceremony. That is when he will take charge of the throne and the crown. Only the queen knows that something will be missing from that ceremony." He lowered his voice and added, "Well, the queen . . . and someone else."

Stanley and Arthur looked at each other, confused. "What do you mean?" Stanley asked.

The detective continued. "Throughout history, the crown jewels have been an important part of the coronation ceremony. One by one, they are given to the new king or queen. Each one of them stands for one part of the ruler's power. For some time, however, the queen has kept a secret. The set of crown jewels is not complete."

"One of them was stolen?" Arthur asked.

"Not exactly," said Detective Bates. "Usually the crown jewels are locked away, but the royal family may also use them for special occasions. It was after one family wedding that the Windsor Ring vanished. The queen has never laid eyes on it again."

"The Windsor Ring?" Stanley repeated.

"The Windsor Ring," Detective Bates repeated sadly. "It has been treasured by the royal family for centuries. It features an unusual group of gems. A blue sapphire, a white diamond, and a red ruby—now the colors of our British flog."

When the detective glanced at a small flagpole in the corner of the office, Stanley figured out what he was saying. He heard "flog," but Detective Bates was talking about a flag!

"The queen's cousin, Lady Laura, was the one who borrowed the ring. She claims she returned it to the vault after the wedding. Since then, she has been spotted many times wearing a colorful ring. But no one has been able to determine if it is really the missing one."

Detective Bates got to his point. "The queen does not want to embarrass her cousin. But this mystery has gone on long enough! Time is running out, and the queen wants the ring back before the next king is crowned. Stonley, how would you like to go on a spy mission?"

"No fair!" Arthur answered before Stanley could say a word. "I want to go, too!"

Detective Bates put a hand up to stop him. "Your family will stay together at all times," he promised Arthur. "But only Stonley will be working to solve the mystery."

He explained the plan. Or, as he called it, "the plon."

Lady Laura, who lived far outside of London, was making a visit to the city.

She would be attending a formal ball at Buckingham Palace—where the queen lived—with many other members of the royal family.

"If Lady Laura has the ring," Detective Bates said, "this will be the perfect time to wear it. The queen is in poor health, so she will not be attending the ball. No one else knows about the missing ring. Lady Laura will think the coast is clear."

"So . . . where do I come in?" Stanley asked.

"You, Stonley, will be attending the ball," said Detective Bates. "Guests like Lady Laura will think you're there— with your family—as a famous guest."

He paused and added, "I understand you are well known around the world. On account of your being . . . er . . . flot."

Stanley looked modestly at the floor. "A lot of people know who I am," he had to agree.

"You will be the perfect spy!" the detective exclaimed. "No one will guess you are undercover. But as you mingle with the guests, you can keep an eye on Lady Laura. You can get a close look at her jewelry. And if she is wearing an unusual ring, you can use a special tool—which I will give you—to determine if it is truly the Windsor Ring."

Detective Bates looked at Stanley, waiting for his reply. Stanley was excited about the mission, but he couldn't help thinking about the detective's accent. He didn't mean to be rude. He just couldn't stop himself before these words came out of his mouth: "I'd be really glod to do it!"

Detective Bates did not seem to notice, though. He just thumped Stanley on the back and said, "Bright chop! I will see you at the ball."

A "chop," Stanley soon learned, was a chap. That was what English people said instead of "guy." Wherever the Lambchops went in London, someone was calling Stanley a chap.

"There's a fine chap," said a taxi driver, giving Flat Stanley a strange look.

"The queue starts here, young chap," said a ticket seller at Westminster Abbey.

Any English chap, Stanley discovered, knew that a queue was a line.

And the line to get in to Westminster Abbey, a cathedral in the middle of London, was really long. "Do we have to do all this sightseeing today? Can we come here tomorrow instead?" Arthur asked.

"Tomorrow we'll be going to the ball," said Mrs. Lambchop. "We don't have much time to see all the great places in London, and I want us to get in as much as we can." So the family waited a whole hour to get in, and Stanley was glad they did.

Westminster Abbey was a huge church with soaring ceilings and stained glass windows. Stanley figured that at least twenty double-decker buses could fit inside, although they might have trouble parking with so many stone pillars in the way.

Mr. Lambchop led the family inside. "Westminster Abbey is one of the biggest churches in London," he explained. "It is also where a lot of history actually happened."

It turned out that every English king or queen had been crowned in Westminster Abbey for over a thousand years. And that coronation ceremony Detective Bates had mentioned? It took place right here! Stanley could hardly believe it.

Someday soon, the new king would sit on the wooden throne—a large, engraved chair, really—that stood in a quiet corner of Westminster Abbey. For the ceremony, he would need all of the crown jewels, including the Windsor Ring.

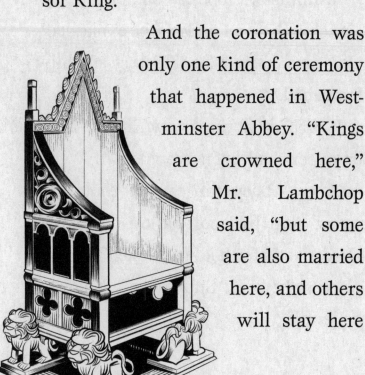

And the coronation was only one kind of ceremony that happened in Westminster Abbey. "Kings are crowned here," Mr. Lambchop said, "but some are also married here, and others will stay here

forever! Kings, queens, soldiers, writers, scientists, leaders . . . lots of them are buried right in the walls and the floor of the cathedral."

Arthur shuddered. "They're buried here?" he repeated. "That is so creepy!"

"Anyone up for a scavenger hunt?" said Mr. Lambchop. He handed each of the boys a list of famous tombs they could find. It *was* pretty creepy, Stanley had to admit. But it was also beautiful. There were dozens of names on the list, and as they searched for some of the tombs, they saw the wonderful architecture and glass windows throughout the cathedral.

But Westminster Abbey was not

nearly as creepy as their next stop, the Tower of London.

The Tower of London was best known for being a terrible jail!

It was not that tall, but it had thick stone walls and sat at the edge of a river. Stanley imagined that the Tower would be hard to attack and easy to defend. Maybe that was why it was a good place to keep things locked up.

"Years ago, prisoners were locked in the Tower," Mr. Lambchop said as they walked through.

"That's correct," their tour guide said. "But today, the crown jewels are kept there. They are on display for visitors to see, protected by thick glass and many guards.

"And the crown jewels are not all jewels, either, but also other objects that had meaning for the royal family. Swords, trumpets, robes," she said. "Plus crowns, of course." She led the family to the glass cases, where the jewels glittered under bright lights.

Stanley's jaw dropped when he saw them. There was a crown encrusted with brilliant gems. There was an ancient sword that looked so sharp, no one would believe it was not brand-new. Stanley could see why these things would be important for anyone, especially a king or queen. It wasn't just that they were priceless. It was that each one also had a long history, connecting a new monarch to the past.

Without the Windsor Ring, though, a link in that chain was missing. It was up to Stanley Lambchop to fix it!

Getting Ready

Stanley loved sightseeing, but he couldn't wait to start his mission. And there was one important thing to do before he could attend a ball at Buckingham Palace. He had to find something to wear!

The next morning, Mr. Lambchop led the way down a long escalator that took the family beneath the city of London.

"Welcome to the Underground!" he said.

Arthur looked at the tunnel ahead of him. "Yes, we are definitely underground," he agreed. "But this does not look like a place to buy clothes."

Mr. Lambchop laughed. "That is because this is the way to the store," he explained.

Stanley noticed something as his eyes adjusted to the light. This was not just any tunnel. It was a train tunnel!

"The London Underground is the city's subway," Mrs. Lambchop told the boys. "Some people also call it the Tube."

Soon Stanley could feel a gust of wind

coming from the end of the tunnel. He grabbed on to Arthur to steady himself as he saw a silver subway train gliding into the station. The doors opened, and people stepped out of the train. A voice came over a loudspeaker. "Mind the gap!" it said.

Mind the gop, Stanley heard. The announcer sounded a lot like Detective Bates.

"What does that mean?" asked Arthur. "What gap?"

"The space between the train and the platform," said Mrs. Lambchop.

Stanley looked down and saw a small, thin gap, which he could easily slip through. Carefully, he stepped into the train, making sure he did not fall into that space. But he had a much bigger problem than the gap! The Tube was very crowded. There were people in every seat, plus people standing in every inch of space between the seats. They were holding on to poles and bars, making a web with their arms. Their feet made a maze on the floor.

"Excuse me," Arthur said politely, edging into a tiny spot.

"Pardon me," Mrs. Lambchop said as she reached above her head for a bar to hold on to.

Stanley slipped past a woman who was reading a magazine. He hopped over a briefcase that was sitting on

the   floor.   By

the time the train

started   moving   again,   he

was leaning against the wall, blend-

ing into an advertising poster. He was

quite comfortable, because he did not

take up much room.

"Look!" said someone in the crowd.

"Flat Stanley is performing in the

Royal Theatre!" Suddenly everyone was looking at him. Well, actually they were looking at the poster behind him.

Stanley turned around to see it. It was an advertisement for an exciting new show. The way he was standing, it looked like he would be acting in the show himself!

When he twisted, though, people could see they weren't looking at a picture of Flat Stanley. They were looking at the *real* Flat Stanley!

"In person, you are even flotter than I expected," someone said.

"May I have your autograph?" someone else asked.

Stanley smiled. He was used to

being famous by now. After all, that was why he was in London in the first place! No one would ever suspect him of attending a palace ball with a secret plan. But he did have one regret about his mission. The thing he was famous for—being flat—had nothing to do with the job. Sometimes being flat was useful. On this trip to London, being flat was just . . . flat.

When the train stopped, the Lambchops went up another long escalator and made their way through the crowded streets to a huge department store called Harrods. As its glass doors swung open, the family stepped into a different world.

The air smelled like perfume, and the floor was as shiny as ice.

Mr. Lambchop looked at a map. "This way to the children's section," he said.

The children's section was full of fancy clothes. These were the kinds of clothes that movie stars wore, Stanley thought. Or maybe models. There was nothing that looked comfortable in sight. He wished he could wear his favorite sweatshirt, or a pair of jeans, to the ball.

"Oh, hello! Can I help you?" A saleswoman looked Stanley over, a little perplexed. "What size would this young gentleman take?" she asked Mrs. Lambchop.

"I think a ten," said Stanley's mother. "Extra thin."

"Is this outfit for a special occasion?" the saleswoman asked Mrs. Lambchop.

"We are attending a ball at Buckingham Palace," Mrs. Lambchop explained.

"How lovely!" said the saleswoman. "You must be very special to be going to a ball. And at Buckingham Palace, no less!"

It took a little while, but she found a suit in Stanley's size. It was a pair of gray pants with a white shirt, a gray vest and jacket, and a black tie. She suggested a pair of black shoes to match.

Stanley struggled to button up the shirt. The sleeves of the jacket were too long. His father had to help him with the tie, and the shoes were so stiff that Stanley could hardly walk in them. When he looked in the mirror, though, he had to admit he looked like he belonged at a ball in a palace. He looked like a Very Important Person.

Meanwhile, Arthur gazed intently at a toy display. The saleswoman turned to Mrs. Lambchop. "Will he be needing a new suit as well?" she asked.

Arthur spoke up right away. "Oh, no . . . that's okay . . . ," he sputtered.

"No way. If I need to wear a suit, so do you!" Stanley dragged his brother from the toys to the suits. By the time they were done with shopping, the boys

had matching outfits. When they stood
side by side, Arthur said, "We look like
twins!" Except that one twin was flat,
and one was not, Stanley thought.

Mrs. Lambchop smiled. "Once you
change back into your regular clothes,
we'll go for tea," she told the boys.

"Harrods is known for its elegant tea-room!"

Stanley and Arthur changed, and a few minutes later, the Lambchop family walked into a beautiful room with all their shopping bags. As soon as they sat down, a waiter asked that funny question again: "Would you like a spot of tea?"

It turned out in England that meant "Would you like a little tea?" Stanley did not want to *drink* any tea. But he did want to *eat* tea, because in England that was the name of a big afternoon snack! Mr. and Mrs. Lambchop poured steaming tea from a pot while Stanley and Arthur helped themselves to the tray of treats that came with it.

Arthur picked up a little sandwich and took a bite. "A cucumber sandwich?" he said. "I've never heard of that, but it's not bad!"

Stanley sliced open a warm scone and spread jam all over it. "Mmmm, tasty," he said. Some of the jam overflowed onto his fingers, and he licked it off.

Quickly, he looked at his mother, but she had not noticed. Just this once, he got away with being impolite.

Someone else had noticed, though. A lady was sitting next to the Lambchops, sitting up very straight in her chair. When she saw Stanley licking his fingers, she took the napkin off her lap and dabbed her lips carefully. She caught his eye and nodded. Was she sending a message? he wondered. Was she reminding him to use a napkin?

The lady was having tea with a girl about Stanley's age. The girl picked up a fork and a knife. "No, Lucy, not like that," the lady said, pinching her lips together. With her own fork and knife, she showed Lucy the right way to cut her food.

Lucy was supposed to be watching the demonstration.

Instead, she was watching Stanley. Her eyes grew large and she covered her mouth in surprise. "Auntie, look," she exclaimed, pointing right at him. "It's Flat St—!"

She did not even get to finish her sentence because Auntie threw her napkin on the table. Her voice was not loud, but it sounded as pinched as her lips. "You must never, ever point at a person, Lucy," she said. "That is not proper at all. You must remember your manners!" She sounded upset. "I think we are finished here."

With that, they swept out of the tea-room.

Stanley frowned as he watched them

leave. "That was a little mean, wasn't it?" he asked his family.

Mrs. Lambchop sipped her tea. "It's a tradition in England to use good manners," she said. "Auntie was teaching Lucy the rules. They are good to know, whether you are just having tea or attending a ball at the palace."

Stanley sighed. He felt a little sorry for Lucy. And also a little sorry for himself. Manners were not his specialty. But if manners were a tradition, he would have to use them while he was on his mission. Following that tradition might be the only way for him to fix the other tradition—crowning the new king with *all* the crown jewels.

Welcome to the Palace!

Back at their hotel, the Lambchops got dressed for the ball. Arthur and Stanley put on the suits that made them look like twins, and Mrs. Lambchop put on a sparkly dress. Mr. Lambchop wore a suit, too, but it had a strange jacket. It looked short in the front and long in the back. "It's called a tailcoat," he told the boys.

"Because the back looks like a tail?" Arthur joked.

Nobody joked when they met up with Detective Bates. He was wearing a plaid skirt with knee socks! "It's a called a kilt," he told the boys. "My family is from Scotland. Where we come from, this is what men wear for special occasions." Stanley smiled politely, as if he saw detectives in kilts every day. Lucy's auntie would be proud of his manners, he thought.

Detective Bates led

them out of the hotel and started walking toward the palace. "I will be right there with you the whole time," he explained. "You can count on me to protect you if anything happens. But I will also be acting like a regular guest at the ball."

He put a hand in the pocket of his kilt and drew out a small black tube. "Now, Stonley, this is for you," he said.

Stanley turned it over and flicked on a switch. A thin beam of light came out of one end, almost blinding him.

"It is disguised as a pen, but this tool has a special purpose," Detective Bates explained. "This ultraviolet light can help you detect imitation gem-stones in one glance. Under this light, a real jewel will look clear, but a fake one will have cloudy spots."

"So I should use this if I find the Windsor Ring?" Stanley asked.

"Bright chop!" said Detective Bates. "Yes, you can run a test right there at the ball. The world's best jewelers rely on lights like this one. Maybe Lady Laura has a ring that just happens to look like the Windsor Ring. Or maybe she has stolen the real one from under the queen's nose. Today we will learn the truth!"

Just then, they arrived at a massive gate. Behind it was a stone building with several sets of pillars. "Welcome to Buckingham Palace!" announced Detective Bates. "Headquarters of the royal family, and home of the queen!"

Stanley gulped. It was an impressive building with hundreds of windows, but it was kind of plain.

"Where are the towers?" Arthur asked. "Where is the moat?"

He said just what Stanley was thinking. This was not the way Stanley had expected a palace to look.

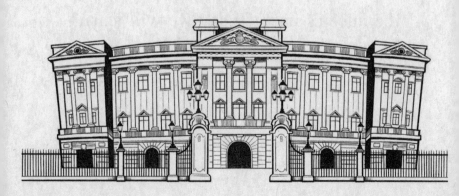

Stanley felt nervous as the gate opened to let them in. Now he knew how to use the ultraviolet light, but how was he supposed to find any jewels in the first place? Detective Bates had not told him much about that. He did not know how to be a spy. He did not even know what people did at a ball!

Detective Bates was ahead of him now, chatting with Mr. Lambchop. Stanley knew that good manners meant he couldn't interrupt with tons of questions. He took a deep breath and pulled himself together. He would try to act natural and keep his eyes open for anything unusual. Any good spy would start with that.

Actually, the first unusual thing was right here in front of him!

There were two men in red coats, like uniforms, with tall black hats. Were the hats made out of fur? Stanley wondered. They looked soft and fuzzy. But the men were a little scary. They stared straight ahead. They did not smile. They did not even move! Stanley noticed they were carrying rifles.

"The Queen's Guard," Detective Bates told Stanley and Arthur. "Protectors of the palace and the queen. They guard the public entrance for visitors and also this private entrance for the guests at the ball."

Stanley shrank away from them

automatically. He hung back behind a lamppost for a second. But Arthur took a big step forward.

"Oh!" said Arthur. "I have heard of these guards. They are not supposed to react to anything they see." He had a twinkle in his eye. "But I bet I can make them smile."

Arthur made a funny face at them. They did not smile.

He clapped his hands so loud that his palms turned red. They did not even blink.

He did a tap dance. He did a cart-wheel. Did they even notice? Stanley wasn't sure. One of the guards had a mustache, and one of them did not. Other than that, they were exactly alike, and neither one had moved a muscle.

Stanley was less frightened once he saw that they were not dangerous. He stepped out from behind the lamppost, ready to walk past the guards and into the palace at last.

But when the guard with the mustache saw Stanley Lambchop, he *moved*! The guard's jaw dropped and his eyes bulged out. Maybe he was not used to seeing flat boys at the palace gate, thought Stanley.

The next second, the guard was stern and still again. But Stanley knew what he had seen.

Sometimes when people asked Stanley for an autograph, he did a little trick to entertain them. If he stood up straight and shook his body, it would ripple, like a sheet on a clothesline or a ribbon in the wind.

Sometimes Stanley liked to act more mature than Arthur, since he was the older brother. Right now, though, he did exactly what his brother did. He tried to make the guards react! He stood in front of the guards and rippled. But the guards didn't budge.

"I saw one of them move before," Stanley told Arthur.

"You did not!" said Arthur. "I don't believe it!"

"I did, too!"

"Boys!" said Mrs. Lambchop. "Enough silliness. Let's get our best manners ready. We are entering the palace!"

Stanley took another deep breath. He couldn't bicker with his brother. He was on a mission for Her Majesty, the queen!

Following Detective Bates, Stanley stepped through the gate, under a stone arch, and into a hallway inside

Buckingham Palace. It was lined with silver mirrors and old paintings of long-ago kings. Stanley felt like he'd been walking for a mile when the hallway opened into a ballroom that had to be the size of a football field.

"Wow," he whispered, looking at Arthur, who also looked surprised. He had never been in a place like this before. It was a little like a museum and a little like a fancy hotel. Everything was gold: the curtains, the chandeliers, even the ceiling. There was a fountain in the middle of the room and a row of tables with heavy platters of food. There were more flowers here than in the Lambchops' whole garden at home, and candles cast a sparkling light on the entire room.

This was how a palace was supposed to look, Stanley thought. This place was fit for a king.

Flat as a Pancake

As they walked through the room, some musicians began to play, and a young man in a tailcoat approached the Lambchops and Detective Bates.

He greeted them warmly. "Welcome," he said in a low voice that Stanley could barely hear over the music. "I'm glad you were able to join us tonight."

Detective Bates turned to Stanley.

"This is Prince Henry," he said. "The future king of England!"

Stanley put two and two together. "Are you the queen's son?" he asked.

He was not sure if this was good manners, but he needed to know. Was Prince Henry the one who needed all the crown jewels?

Prince Henry nodded. "I am!" he said. He smiled at Stanley. "I hope you will enjoy your evening at the palace."

He winked to show he knew that Stanley was here for another reason, too.

"Will you come with me?" he asked. "I will introduce you to a very special guest."

"Remember," Detective Bates whispered, "I am here if you need help. I will never be very far away." He stepped into the crowd with the rest of the Lambchops.

Stanley followed Prince Henry through a group of guests until he came to some women in long gowns, standing by the fountain. One of them had excellent posture. "Lady Laura," said the prince, "there is someone here I'd like you to meet."

Lady Laura! She was the one who had borrowed the Windsor Ring before it disappeared. She could be a thief! Do

I have to shake her hand? Stanley wondered.

When she turned around, Stanley gasped and quickly realized he would have to.

Lady Laura was the woman from the tearoom at Harrods! Lucy's auntie! Stanley knew that Lady Laura cared deeply about good manners, like handshaking.

"A pleasure to meet you," she said. "Charmed, I'm sure." Her smile was frozen and her fingers

were cold. As he shook her hand, Stanley could feel that she was wearing rings, but he did not look at them. He did not want her to guess why he was here quite yet.

"It is very nice to meet you, too," he said.

She asked, "Is this your first visit to London?"

Her voice was friendly enough, but she was not even looking at Stanley. She was looking over his head. Was she trying to find someone else to talk to? Stanley wondered.

Sure enough, Lady Laura caught someone's eye and nodded. "If you'll excuse me . . . ," she said. She drifted away, and Stanley was on his own.

What did people do at a ball? Well, now Stanley would find out. Some people were dancing near the musicians, but more people were just standing around and talking. All around him, he could hear the clink of glasses and the hum of conversation.

The ballroom was full of actors and rock stars and gold medalists—not to mention members of the royal family—so Flat Stanley did not stand out. That was what Detective Bates had in mind, Stanley remembered. Since no one was watching Stanley, he could watch everybody else! It was the first step toward becoming a spy.

A server in an apron approached Stanley, holding out a tray. "Would you care for a canapé?"

Stanley looked at the tray just as his stomach rumbled. There were about a dozen tiny meatballs and a bowl of toothpicks. He said, "Yes, please," and stabbed four of them with a toothpick.

Just when he had stuffed all four

meatballs in his mouth and was savoring the delicious taste, Lady Laura happened to glance his way. He could read the disapproval in her eyes. But the meatballs were so good! And here came another server with another tray!

In a corner of the ballroom, Stanley could see Arthur with a group of children. One of them was Lucy, Lady Laura's niece. It looked like there were things for kids to do over there. They had some arts and crafts and an overflowing trunk full of dress-up clothes. Stanley wondered if they were having fun.

But he was here for one purpose, so he kept an eye on Lady Laura. She did not seem to be doing anything unusual. She took a sip from her glass. She laughed at something. She stood up very straight.

Stanley needed to get a good look at her hands. He was waiting for the perfect moment to move closer, when all of a sudden she was back at his side.

"Are you enjoying the ball?" she asked. It was a friendly question, but she did not look friendly. Her eyes were narrow and her lips were pinched together. What did I ever do to her? Stanley wondered.

Then he had a terrible thought.

What if she knew why he was here?

Had she been watching him, too?

Stanley stood up a little straighter. He could not let his imagination run away with him. Maybe Lady Laura was just uncomfortable around him. Then she asked, "May I ask about your condition? Er, your flatness?" She almost sounded embarrassed.

"Oh, sure. I have been flat for a long time now," said Stanley. "But except for being flat, I'm a normal boy." Right now, being flat did not seem like anything special. It was not even helping Stanley find the Windsor Ring. All he could do was stand here. Lady Laura had her hands behind her back!

"Hmm," said Lady Laura. "Very interesting." When the musicians finally started a new song, she moved toward the dance floor. Now she was waving her hands in the air!

Stanley decided not to let her out of his sight. He did not know how long the ball would last. He could not wait too long to look for the ring.

When the song was over, Lady Laura left the dance floor. She got something to drink. She put on some lipstick.

When she walked down the hallway where Stanley had come in, he followed her at a safe distance. She looked at the paintings. She glanced in a mirror. She was not acting suspicious, and Stanley was about to give up.

Then, all of a sudden, she did something strange.

She turned off the main hallway into a smaller hallway. It looked like it led to the kitchen. She glanced at her watch, as if she were waiting for someone, and it was then that Stanley saw something sparkle on her finger.

Next thing he knew, the person she was waiting for appeared.

And it was the guard Stanley had

seen outside—the one who had moved! Stanley would recognize that mustache anywhere! He wondered where the guard had put his rifle.

The guard and Lady Laura put their heads together and began to whisper. Stanley would have to get a little closer if he wanted to hear them. Could they be talking about the Windsor Ring?

Right now, he was standing out in the open where the two hallways met. He couldn't stay there without the risk of being seen. What if they spotted me already? Stanley wondered. The thought gave him the shivers.

Stanley stood up against the wall of the larger hallway and inched slowly toward the corner. He couldn't see Lady Laura or the guard from this angle, but as he got nearer he could hear them whispering. A little closer, and he would be able to make out the words.

He was kind of scared, but Stanley had to smile. Being famous had helped him blend in at the ball. But being flat was coming in very handy, too! He was almost invisible from the side. In his suit, he even blended into the black-and-white patterned wallpaper!

He was as close as he could get now, and just in time. It seemed like their conversation was about to end.

Lady Laura stepped away from the

guard, but he was still speaking. The guard rubbed his chin, blocking the sound of his voice, but Stanley could understand the last few words: *"Flat as a pancake."*

Stanley turned bright red. His heart started beating quickly. Were they talking about him?

As he stood there, stunned, the two of them turned the corner together. Luckily, they were not looking in his direction. But he was looking in theirs, and what he saw made his heart beat even faster.

Lady Laura's ring was red, white, and blue. It sparkled like fireworks, even in the dim light of the hallway.

Was it really the Windsor Ring? Stanley knew he had the equipment to answer that question. But could he figure it out before they caught him?

Stanley Lambchop, Super Spy

When they were out of sight, Stanley walked back up the hallway and into the ballroom. He thought hard about what to do next.

One thing was clear. Stanley could not just walk up to Lady Laura and test her ring. She would suspect what he was up to. Maybe she suspected already! Why else would she be talking to the guard about Stanley?

Stanley Lambchop was not an expert spy, but he knew a few things. A spy was supposed to be prepared for anything. A spy was supposed to think on his feet. He needed another plan. And he needed a little help.

Stanley did not want to ask his mother or father. What kind of spy relied on his parents?

Detective Bates was still here somewhere, but Stanley did not want anyone to know he was working with Scotland Yard.

Luckily, there was another person Stanley could count on. He had wanted to be a part of the mission from the very beginning! Stanley headed over to Arthur.

Arthur was in the middle of a group of children, playing charades. "We are supposed to keep quiet," he told Stanley in a low voice.

Lady Laura's niece added, "Children should be seen and not heard." Her auntie had probably taught her that rule, Stanley thought. Good manners were no fun!

He scanned the kids' corner of the ballroom. He saw pads of paper and crayons, games and toys, and that giant trunk of costumes. Stanley smiled.

Sometimes a spy had to use his imagination.

He took a step away and motioned for Arthur to follow. "How is it going?" Arthur asked.

"Shhh," said Stanley. "I need some help."

"Really?" Arthur's face lit up. "What can I do?" he asked.

Stanley looked at the box of costumes. "How would you feel about dressing up?" he asked.

A little while later, Stanley lingered at the edge of the dance floor while Arthur made his way toward Lady Laura. Not that anyone would know it was Arthur.

His suit was now hidden in the Buckingham Palace bathroom. And instead, Arthur was wearing the same outfit as the servers who were passing the trays. He was all in black, with an apron tied around his neck and waist.

Anyone who looked carefully would notice that the pants were rolled up because they were much too long.

Anyone who looked carefully would see that Arthur's apron was the wrong color, since it was really just a costume.

But no one was looking carefully.

The guests were enjoying the ball!

A good spy never broke his cover. So, while Arthur did his job—walking through the crowd, toward the ring— Stanley's job was to act like nothing had changed. He was just a famous flat boy, here to mingle with royalty and enjoy the ball.

When a well-known actress asked Stanley to dance, of course he said yes! "You were in my favorite movie," he told her as he twirled. "I am your biggest fan!"

Every time he spun around, he could see the guard standing against the wall on the edge of the ballroom. Was he watching Stanley? Was he waiting for Lady Laura to join him again? Had he noticed Arthur? His expression was hidden by his mustache.

Stanley tried not to worry. He pretended everything was totally normal.

"I am your biggest fan, too, Flat Stanley," the actress said when the song was over. She kissed him on the cheek to say good-bye.

Stanley checked on Arthur. He was moving very slowly.

So, what else would Stanley do if

he were just here for fun? He would definitely check out the dessert table, he decided. He found a large plate and piled it high with possibilities. Cookies, a slice of cake, a tart, a brownie . . . Stanley would sample one of each.

"Got your pudding sorted, Stonley?" said a voice beside him. It was Detective Bates! "Huh?" As usual, Stanley was not sure what he meant. There was no pudding on the dessert table. He wasn't sorting anything at all.

Detective Bates grinned. "I mean, have you decided what to have for dessert?"

He could speak the same English as Stanley! Sometimes even the best spies were surprised.

"Oh, yes, *everything* is sorted," Stanley told him meaningfully. He hoped Detective Bates understood his double meaning. He was talking about his dessert and his mission at the same time. The plan was moving ahead.

Just then, from the corner of his eye, Stanley saw Arthur get to Lady Laura at last. Stanley left his dessert with Detective Bates. It was time to join his brother!

Like all the servers at the ball, Arthur was carrying a tray. But there was nothing to eat on the tray. There was just a folded piece of paper.

"Excuse me, ma'am?" said Arthur to Lady Laura. (It came out as "mom," because he was using his best English accent.) "I have an important message for you."

Lady Laura wheeled around. "Pardon?" she said. She looked Arthur up and down.

"I have a special delivery. An urgent message."

She stood up a little straighter, almost like she had been waiting for news.

Arthur fumbled in his apron. "But first you need to sign for it . . ."

He produced a small clipboard.

Stanley and Arthur had found it in the dress-up box.

Arthur patted his pockets. "Now I just need to find my pen."

Stanley knew that Arthur did not have a pen. This line was his cue to get ready.

He took a step closer for a clear look at the ring on Lady Laura's finger. Stanley thought, I would have noticed it even if I wasn't on a spy mission! It was the biggest ring he had ever seen, and it flashed with every move she made. The red, white, and blue reflected the brilliant light from the ballroom's chandeliers.

Stanley was excited. It certainly

looked like it could be the Windsor Ring! In a moment, he would test it to be sure.

Meanwhile, Arthur was still pretending to look for something to write with. Carefully, he checked all of his pockets. Then he checked them all over again.

Lady Laura was getting impatient. She put on her glasses, and the ring flashed. She brushed some lint off her dress, and the ring flashed. She glared at Arthur. "May I just read the message?" she said coolly.

"The sender insists on your signature, ma'am," said Arthur. He held his

lips in a tight line. Was he trying not to laugh? If he laughed, Arthur would ruin everything!

It was time for the real spy to step in.

"I have a pen," Stanley volunteered quickly, as if he had just arrived and noticed they needed help. "Would you like to borrow it?"

"Please," said Lady Laura.

She did not meet Stanley's eyes as she reached for the pen. She did not even look at the pen. Did she think it was beneath her? Did she think it was improper?

Whatever the problem was, Stanley was glad she was distracted. Because the thing he was handing over was not a pen at all. It was the ultraviolet flashlight from Scotland Yard!

Lady Laura moved her hand toward Stanley's hand, and he flicked the switch.

Suddenly a blinding light was focused on her ring!

Twin Rings

Shocked by the beam of light, the guard sprang into action and thundered toward Stanley, Arthur, and Lady Laura. "What is the meaning of this?" he bellowed. He pushed Lady Laura out of the way and stood in front of Stanley. "I demand an explanation!"

Lady Laura blinked. She did not know what had happened. "I just want to read the message," she told Arthur in a tight voice. She did not understand—yet—that it had all been a trick.

Arthur looked at his feet. He looked to Stanley for help. He knew the "message" was just a paper with some scribbles on it.

Stanley was still reeling from the message *he* had received from the ultraviolet light. In disbelief, he gripped the flashlight in his hand. Lady Laura was not wearing the Windsor Ring after all. The light had revealed some cloudy spots on the red, white, and blue stones. Now Stanley knew it was a perfect fake.

His mission had failed.

He would not be able to return the

missing crown jewel to the queen or—someday—to the new king.

Stanley sighed. He decided to be honest. Well, mostly honest. "I am here on a mission," he explained to Lady Laura and the guard. "My brother is only trying to help. We have been looking for some stolen property."

The guard's eyes bulged out, just as they had when he first spotted Stanley. "Yes, I have purchased some property," he said.

Stanley looked at his brother. What did that have to do with anything?

Maybe, with his furry hat, the guard had not heard quite right?

Lady Laura stood up even straighter

than before. "I know it is unusual," she explained, "for a member of the Queen's Guard to do business with a member of the royal family, but it is true. I have sold him a plot of land."

Stanley felt like he had wandered into the wrong conversation.

Arthur looked like he was about to laugh again.

Just then, Detective Bates arrived. He showed his badge from Scotland Yard. "I hove been working with Stonley Lombchop," he told Lady Laura and the guard. "He has been on a special assignment for the queen. Now could you tell me more about this . . . property?"

The guard spoke up. "It's a beautiful spot, sir. Perfect for my farm. Many acres for the sheep to graze. And plenty of space for planting, too. No trees and flat as a pancake."

Now Stanley was the one who almost laughed. The guard and Lady Laura had not been talking about him at all! They had been talking about a piece of land!

Detective Bates continued. "Very well, sir," he told the guard. "But yours is not the property in question. We are searching for a missing ring."

Arthur could not help himself. He pointed right at Lady Laura's finger. "A ring that looks like that one!"

"But we know that's not it!" Stanley

pointed out in a hurry.

"Are you familiar with the Windsor Ring?" Detective Bates asked the guard and Lady Laura. "It appears that your ring is its twin. And there's been a . . . misunderstanding."

Lady Laura stood up a little straighter. "Oh, I think I understand just perfectly," she said, scowling. "You thought I was a thief!"

Now they were attracting quite a crowd. Mr. and Mrs. Lambchop had arrived. So had Lucy, Lady Laura's niece.

Lady Laura wrapped a protective arm around the girl. Then her eyes filled with tears.

"You thought I was a thief," repeated Lady Laura, "because *everyone* thinks I am a thief. But I never stole the Windsor Ring. The truth is much worse than that. I *lost* it!"

Detective Bates gasped. "How did you lose it, ma'am?"

"I wore it to a family wedding," said Lady Laura. "Right here in this very ballroom!"

She paused to catch her breath.

"Then I never saw it again! And I could never admit I had lost one of the crown jewels, you understand. So I made up a different story."

Stanley couldn't believe it. In her

own way, Lady Laura was undercover, too!

"A skilled jeweler made me a copy of the Windsor Ring. I made sure that members of the royal family saw me wearing it. I let them think I had taken a crown jewel! My reputation was ruined, and I had to sell some of my land. I have kept my secret, but I have never stopped looking for the real ring. Somehow we must find it before a new king is crowned!"

As Lady Laura spoke, Lucy broke away from the group. Stanley was surprised her auntie didn't stop her.

Maybe Lady Laura was not as mean

as she had seemed at first. Maybe her perfect manners had just been covering up her worry about the ring? But even Stanley thought it was rude for Lucy to start playing while Lady Laura was sharing her terrible secret.

Lucy sat down and drew a picture.

Detective Bates was still trying to follow the story. "Do you remember taking off the Windsor Ring?" he asked Lady Laura.

"I was wearing it throughout the wedding," said Lady Laura. "But when I put my coat on to leave, it was gone."

Lucy piped up with a question of her own. "Was it cold that day?" she asked.

Lady Laura looked blankly at her. "It

was January," she said. "It was probably cold."

"Were you wearing a hat?" asked Lucy.

Lady Laura sighed. "I don't remember. And why on earth does it matter?"

"Because you might also have been wearing gloves," said Lucy. "Like these." She held up the picture she'd just drawn of some embroidered gloves.

"Oh yes," said Lady Laura. "I used to have a pair of gloves like those. Yes, I suppose I could have worn them that night. But . . . how did you know?"

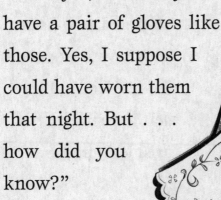

From the costume box, Lucy took a pair of gloves that matched her picture. "Because the gloves are still here," she said. "After all that time. Someone must have thought they were for children. I put them on while we were playing before. And I noticed there was something stuck inside one of the fingers!"

"I might have left my gloves at the wedding," mused Lady Laura. Her eyes opened wide. "Could I have left the ring behind, inside them?"

Lucy handed the gloves to Lady Laura. They were a little dusty with age, but she recognized them right away.

Then Lucy reached into the box one more time. She took out a spectacular ring, shining red, white, and blue.

"Here's the thing that was stuck inside," she said. "Does it belong to you?"

High Above London

Lady Laura gasped. She held the ring in her fingers and gazed at it as light bounced all around. This ring flashed even more than the imitation ring that was still on her finger. Its red, white, and blue stones were as clear as water and as radiant as the sun.

"One of the genuine crown jewels,"

said Mrs. Lambchop. "Part of England's history." She shook her head in wonder.

"It will be back where it belongs," said Mr. Lambchop. "Ready for the next coronation, whenever that is."

Stanley took out his flashlight again. He was still thinking like a spy! "We should test it to be sure it's the real one."

"How about I hold it, just for safe-keeping?" said the guard. He held the ring up so the entire group could see Stanley cover it in ultravio-let light. This time

there were no clouds in the stones. Stanley could see the beam of light pierce the gems and come out on the other side!

Detective Bates shook Stanley's hand. "Well done, Stonley, old chop!"

Lady Laura smiled for the first time since Stanley had met her at Harrods. Her manners were still very formal, though. "I am quite grateful to you, Stanley," she said. "Now everyone will know the truth."

"You're welcome," Stanley said automatically.

"You're welcome," Arthur added. "Now, can I get out of this costume? I don't love wearing a suit, but anything is better than wearing this apron!"

No one had thanked Arthur, but Stanley would thank him later. He had thought that being a spy would be a job for only him, but it turned out he needed a whole team—Detective Bates and Lucy and especially his brother—to find the Windsor Ring. It was kind of like his flatness, Stanley thought. Being flat had helped him on his spy mission, but it was not the only tool he needed. It also helped to be famous. It also helped to be quick on his feet!

Speaking of quick . . .

Stanley raced back to the plate of

desserts he had left behind. And it was still in the same place!

And then, before the ball was over, he rushed back to the dance floor. No one could dance quite like a flat kid, after all! He flapped and rippled his body in time to the music until the last musicians packed up to go home. The ball at Buckingham Palace would always have a bright place in Stanley's memory, shining like the Windsor Ring.

* * *

The next morning, soon after the Lambchop family woke up, Mrs. Lambchop noticed something near the door of their hotel room. "What is this?" she asked. She took a thick white envelope off the floor.

"Can I see?" Arthur asked, grabbing it out of her hand. "Oh, it's an invitation!"

Stanley yanked it away from his brother and read it out loud:

Her Majesty the Queen requests the honour of your presence this morning at the Changing of the Guard, Buckingham Palace.

The Changing of the Guard, it turned out, was a huge parade in front of Buckingham Palace. One group of the Queen's Guard marched in, with a band leading the way, and replaced the group that had been guarding the palace since the night before. There was a large crowd watching the ceremony. Stanley was not sure why they had needed an invitation.

Stanley stood wedged between two visitors with cameras, straining to catch a glimpse of the one guard he knew. "I wonder if we'll see the guard from the ball," he mused.

"How would you ever spot him?" said Mrs. Lambchop. "All the guards look exactly the same!"

Sure enough, though, Stanley knew him by his mustache. He was one of the guards leaving the palace after night duty. Stanley watched him march toward the new guards and inspect them. Stanley watched him keep time with the drums and bugles, heading away from the palace for some rest. Then, to Stanley's surprise, the guard winked as he passed the Lambchops! He moved his head just enough that Stanley realized the guard was giving him a message.

"I think he wants us to follow him!" Stanley told his family.

Mr. Lambchop frowned. "How could you know that?" he asked.

"Just watch him!" Stanley insisted. "He's moving his chin in the direction he wants us to go."

Mr. and Mrs. Lambchop had their doubts, but they agreed to do it. They followed the guard and his regiment all the way around the palace, where there were fewer observers. The guard was leaving with his group, but he glanced back at Stanley one more time and pointed his chin toward the sky.

Stanley looked in the direction he was pointing. The sky was bright blue over the city, but there was nothing else there—not even a cloud. When Stanley lowered his gaze, though, he wondered if there was something he was supposed to be seeing on the palace itself. The roof? Then—*oh!*— he knew just what it was. A balcony! With a figure standing there, waving at the few selected observers below. Maybe this was what the invitation was for?

"Can I borrow your binoculars?" Stanley asked his mother.

He put them to his eyes and focused carefully.

Then he knew for sure why they were here.

It was a special gathering to see a special someone. A royal someone. The queen!

She was not well, and she was not young. But she was happy today, because she had Windsor Ring back. It sparkled in the London sun, under the clear blue sky, back where it belonged.

The Lambchops' last stop in London was a giant Ferris wheel on the edge of the river. It was called the London Eye! Instead of seats or booths, the London Eye had glass capsules to carry the passengers. The Lambchops were sealed into a capsule with two other families, and the towering wheel carried them high above the city.

"There's Big Ben!" Arthur called out.

"There's Scotland Yard!" said Mr. Lambchop.

"And the palace!" Mrs. Lambchop added.

They had seen a lot of London in a short time. From this high up, the double-decker buses looked like toys, crawling through the busy streets.

Stanley pressed himself flat against the glass to look. This was the best place to see the whole city, he thought. It was a good place for a visitor. And also a good place for a spy.

Stanley Lambchop kept his eyes wide open, because he was already looking for his next case.

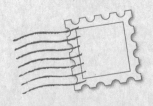

WHAT YOU NEED TO KNOW ABOUT ENGLAND AND THE QUEEN!

1. The tower known as Big Ben was originally named the Clock Tower and then renamed the Elizabeth Tower in 2012 in honor of Queen Elizabeth's Diamond Jubilee, which is equal to 60 years. It is the bell within the tower that is actually named Big Ben.

2. Buckingham Palace has 240 bedrooms for the royals, guests, and staff. There are also 78 bathrooms, 92 offices, and 19 state rooms. There are 775 total rooms!

3. In 1671, a man named "Colonel" Thomas Blood attempted to steal the Crown Jewels by knocking the

Keeper of the Regalia unconscious and taking several items. He was almost successful until the son of the keeper arrived and sounded the alarm.

4. The British Flag is also called the "Union Jack."

5. The British love tea so much that over 60 billion cups are consumed each year—that's more than 900 cups per person.

6. Fish and chips is a traditional British meal. It is made by frying battered cod and served with chunky fried potatoes called "chips."

7. Queen Elizabeth I had a large wardrobe and was very fashionable. Some estimate that she owned almost 2,000 pairs of gloves.

8. The London Eye is a giant observation wheel that stretches 443 feet high. It is the most popular paid tourist attraction in Great Britain and has more than 3.5 million people visit every year.

9. England has a longstanding tradition of monarchy going back over 1,500 years, with 66 rulers over that time period.

10. The melody of the British national anthem, "God Save the Queen," is the same as the melody from the United States song "My Country 'Tis of Thee."

11. London is one of the most crowded cities in England.

12. Queen Elizabeth II is the longest reigning monarch in British history.

13. The Tower of London also housed a Royal Menagerie that existed for more than 600 years and contained animals like lions, tigers, elephants, and even kangaroos.

14. The currency of Britain is the United Kingdom Pound, which uses £ as its symbol.

15. Officers of the London police force are nicknamed "bobbies."